KU-793-502

For Emily and Giles Woolley

First published 1985 by Walker Books Ltd,
87 Vauxhall Walk, London SE11 5HJ

This edition produced 2000 for The Book People Ltd
Hall Wood Avenue, Haydock, St Helens WA11 9UL

2 4 6 8 10 9 7 5 3 1

© 1985 Shirley Hughes

This book has been typeset in Vendome.

Printed in Hong Kong

British Library Cataloguing in Publication Data
A catalogue record for this book is
available from the British Library.

ISBN 0-7445-6739-4

Noisy

Shirley Hughes

TED SMART

Noisy noises!

Pan lids clashing,

Dog barking,
Plate smashing,

Telephone ringing,

Baby bawling,

Midnight cats

Cat-a-wauling,

Door slamming,

Aeroplane zooming,

Vacuum cleaner
Vroom-vroom-vrooming,

And if I dance and sing a tune,
Baby joins in with a saucepan and spoon.

Gentle noises ...

Dry leaves swishing,

Falling rain,
Splashing, splishing,

Rustling trees,
Hardly stirring,

Lazy cat
Softly purring.

Story's over,
Bedtime's come,

Crooning baby
Sucks his thumb.

All quiet, not a peep,

Everyone is
fast asleep.